The School Play Surprise

By Gail Herman
Illustrated by Duendes del Sur

SCHOLASTIC INC.
New York   Toronto   London   Auckland   Sydney
Mexico City   New Delhi   Hong Kong   Buenos Aires

ISBN-10: 0-439-78809-9
ISBN-13: 978-0-439-78809-0

12 11 10 9 8 7 6 5 4   40   9 10 11/0

Designed by Michael Massen
Printed in the U.S.A.
First printing, January 2007

Scooby-Doo and Shaggy were waiting
outside Coolsville High.
"Like, where is everybody?" asked Shaggy.

Classes were over. Lights were turned off.
School buses were pulling away. Fred, Velma,
and Daphne were nowhere in sight.

Shaggy checked his watch.

"Like, that new pizza place isn't going to stay open much longer," he said. "We need to find the gang."

Shaggy pushed open the heavy doors. The school was quiet. Everything looked different in the dark.

"Man, this is spooky," Shaggy whispered.

Scooby took a small step forward.
His nails clicked loudly on the floor. He
jumped back in fear.

"Come on, good buddy," Shaggy urged. "This is for pizza."

"Rizza!" said Scooby. He moved inside. Shaggy followed and —

Bang!

The doors slammed shut behind them.

"Nothing scary here!" Shaggy tried to convince himself. "It's just school."
Thud!
Something crashed.

"Let's find the gang and get out of here," Shaggy said.

Faint voices drifted down the hall. They were coming from the theater.

Shaggy and Scooby tiptoed toward the theater. The voices grew loud and angry. Something was going on.

Scooby pushed against the doors. They didn't budge. Something was blocking them. *GRRR!*
"It's a wild animal!" exclaimed Shaggy.

Scooby rubbed his tummy. "Rungry!"
"Oh, that noise is your stomach!"
Shaggy said. "We've got to get that
pizza!"

They pushed again. Just at that moment, the doors swung open. Shaggy and Scooby tumbled onto the theater floor.

Velma stared down at them.
She looked mad.
   "Leave now! While you have
the chance!" she hissed.

Velma slipped out the side door.
"Like, why that crazy warning?" asked Shaggy.
Just then they heard a scream. It was coming from backstage.
AHHHH!
"It's Raphne!" yelped Scooby.

Suddenly, Fred stepped into view. He was pacing back and forth. A heavy black cape hung from his shoulders. His skin was ghostly white.

"Velma!" he called in a hoarse voice. "Let's begin!"

"Zoinks!" said Shaggy. "Fred looks like a vampire!"

Slowly, Shaggy and Scooby crept forward. In the distance, Daphne screamed again.

A moment later, Velma pushed Daphne close to Fred. Daphne struggled, kicking her legs. "No, no, no!" Daphne cried.

Fred edged closer. He loomed over
Daphne.

"I'm desperate," he croaked. "I need to
drink your —"

"Oh!" Daphne gasped, and fainted.

"Fred is a vampire!" Shaggy cried. "And Velma, too! We have to rescue them all!" Scooby turned to run — the other way.

"But if we rescue them we can get pizza!" added Shaggy.

In a flash, Shaggy and Scooby raced back to their friends.

Fred reached for Daphne. . . .

"Stay away from her, Fred," Shaggy warned.

Fred turned to them.

"Like, stay away from her, please," Shaggy added.

"Hi, guys," said Fred. "You should stay away from me. This costume is making me so hot. I might faint, too. I really need a drink."

"You need a drink of blood?" Shaggy asked, shaking.

Fred gave him a funny look. "Water. Daphne has some in her backpack."

"I had such a bad case of stage fright that I fainted!" Daphne said.

Velma glared at Shaggy and Scooby.
"I told you two to leave! This is a rehearsal.
No audience!"

"Uh, so, like, this is a play?" Shaggy realized. "The cape is a costume? Fred's pale because he's hot and thirsty? Daphne just has stage fright?"

"What did you think?" asked Velma. "That Fred was a vampire? This is a romantic play, and I'm the director." She held out the script.

"Hmm," said Shaggy. "*Looking for Love*. I know where to find that."

"I love this pizza!" Shaggy told the gang. "And look at Daphne!" said Velma. "Now that she's used to an audience, her stage fright is cured!"

"Bravo, Daphne!" cried Shaggy.
"Ravo, rizza!" cried Scooby.